© 2022 All rights reserved. No part of this publication may be reproduced, scanned distributed, or transmitted in any form or by any means, including photocopying, recording, or other electronic or mechanical methods, without the prior written permission of the publisher, except in the case of brief quotations embodied in critical reviews and certain other noncommercial uses permitted by copyright law. Thank you for buying an authorized edition of this book and for complying with copyright laws.

Manufactured in the United States

Any resemblance to actual events or persons, living or dead, is entirely coincidental. This is in no form meant for harm nor do we promote harm. Personal perspective use only. Please do not copy/mimic any words or illustration from this book.

Illustrations by Cameron Wilson for Soulsimplicity Design and Publishing.

MAMAS APOLOGIZE TOO....

A BOOK ABOUT ACCOUNTABILITY AND A MESSAGE FOR PARENTS

BY CANDI PURDIMAN
ILLUSTRATED BY CAMERON WILSON

"Madi, stop running!"
"Riley, stop yelling!"

"Christian, I told you to get off of your game!"

"Malia, sit down!" Mom yelled in frustration.

"Why do I have to say the same thing every single day? Madalin you are ten and Christian you are seven, so I expect for you to act that way. I should not have to get on you the same way I do Malia and Riley, whose two and three. Everyone just go to your rooms!"

"Candi you must remember that although they are the oldest, they are still kids." Malinda replied.

"I know but they understand right from wrong," said Candi.

"What else is going on because you usually have more patience than this? She asked concerned.

"Today just hasn't been a good day. First I woke up late for work and on the way to work my tire busted, I had to wait three hours until the tow company came which caused me to miss an important meeting about my books:" Madalin learns how to pray" and "Grandma is An Angel now," I finally get home and the stove isn't working, baby Caison started screaming to the top of his lungs because he wanted a bottle, and to top it off the kids weren't listening!"

"Wow, it all makes sense! Everything that went wrong today, you took that out on the kids which is totally unacceptable. None of that is their fault. I understand you're overwhelmed but as parents we must learn to separate our emotions. We can't teach our children to control their emotions, if we haven't taught ourselves."

"You are absolutely right I'll call you back; I'm going to apologize!"

"Madalin, Christian, Riley, and Malia come downstairs please!"

"Yes mama," they all said together.

"I just want to apologize for getting frustrated and yelling. I had a really bad day and I accidentally took that out on you and that is not okay. It is okay to have a bad day and to even get upset but you should not take it out on another person. When we are upset we should take a minute to calm down."

"Mama when we are upset, what can we do to calm ourselves down?"

"Can we practice that mama?" Madalin questioned.

"Can we practice that mama?" Madalin questioned.

"I think we got it, I can remember that! Apology accepted!" Madalin said.

CPSIA information can be obtained
at www.ICGtesting.com
Printed in the USA
LVHW071436271222
736006LV00002B/36